A CALL IN THE NIGHT
AND OTHER STORIES

A CALL IN THE NIGHT

AND OTHER STORIES

GABRIELLE LEIMON

Grist Books 2014

Editor Michael Stewart

Editorial Team Hannah Batley, Elizabeth Cavanagh, Alexandra Hopwood, Charlotte Thompson

Cover Design Kagayaku Ink

Inner Page Design Carnegie Book Production

A Call In The Night is published by Grist Books.

Please note that all work published here is previously unpublished.

www.hud.ac.uk/grist

Grist Books is supported entirely by The University of Huddersfield and would not exist without this support. We would like to take the opportunity to express our gratitude for this continuing support.

ISBN: 978-0-9563099-5-2

University of
HUDDERSFIELD
Inspiring tomorrow's professionals

For my father, mother and sister for inspiring and encouraging me at every turn.

For Hannah and all the cups of tea that fuelled this work.

For Michael Stewart and Simon Crump for setting rules and then encouraging me to break them.

Contents

The Gift of a Dying Father   1

A Call In The Night   7

Creep   13

One   15

The Gift of a Dying Father

I T SEEMED SO strange that one life should begin just as another was ending. It was only a few weeks after Casper was diagnosed with cancer that his wife Celia discovered she was pregnant. They had been trying to conceive for so long they had thought they'd never be blessed with children. The doctor, voice cold and hands clasped, told Casper he only had a few years. The words seemed rehearsed, said before many times over to thousands of patients, with a learned sense of sympathy. Casper and Celia had to sit down and have the necessary conversations. They discussed funerals for someone still living and holidays they could take to enjoy the 'time they had left'.

Over time Casper's hands were less red from daily life and butter pale as the life drained from him with each passing morning. It seemed that, bit by bit, parts of him were leaving and going to wherever it is we end up next.

When Celia gave birth it was a bittersweet moment. Casper, hands fumbling and brow sweating at the prospect of becoming a father, felt so useless. There was a strong pressure to be as good as possible in whatever time he had in this role. The moment he held Daniel in his arms was a moment of truth, joy and pain. Casper knew that time with his son was going to be limited. The newborn kicked and squirmed in his arms before settling down. Daniel had that new baby smell and a tuft of jet black hair. Wrapped in a white blanket and a tiny knitted hat, Casper held him as if trying to absorb every second. He took several pictures of Daniel and had Celia take several of himself holding his son to leave behind as if to remind his family that he had been there.

Later that night, Daniel's first night home, Casper woke up in a haze of fear. He could feel the little specks of tumour growing within him, hungrily absorbing much of him and his remaining energy. They were little entities just wanting their life and happily taking it from him much like how Daniel fed from Celia's breast. This house was full of small things wanting to feed and to grow. The clock by the side of the bed stated that it was five in the morning. Outside the road was dark, street lights off-duty for the night. He sat up alone for some time shrouded in darkness as he contemplated his fate. He began to wonder what he could leave behind for the tiny child coddled in a cot at the foot of the bed. He realised he'd never make it to see his child grow. He'd never see his boy become a man. This thought joined so many others that lined his general consciousness and followed him through his final days.

Casper wandered down the stairs with a strange sense of purpose. Slumping down at his desk he opened a drawer. In it was an untouched pack of Marlboro cigarettes and a small lighter from his biking days. It wasn't like they were going to hurt him now. He curled open the lid of the box, placed a cigarette between his pursed lips, and lit it. The angry orange glow flickered as he inhaled, lungs filling with smoke. Putting pen to paper, he began.

> My Dear Daniel,
> It seems so strange that I should be writing this to you now. Upstairs I just settled you down in your cot. When you open this you will be a man. If you are reading this, I'm dead, son. I wish I wasn't. I wish I could have been able to take you to football practice or give you advice when you took home your first girlfriend. I won't be around when you start to grow a beard so I can show you how to shave. I'm sorry for that. I just feel as if I'll be missing out on so many important milestones in your life. I'm sure that as the man of the house you're looking after your mother and making your Dad proud.

Then Casper took a photo of himself, a photo of Celia and one of Daniel and surfed the internet for a website to predict what a baby would look like as an adult. It was an idea he'd been toying with for some time. If he couldn't watch his child grow up he could still see if technology could provide the next best thing. After finding one, he generated an image of eighteen-year-old Daniel. He had blue eyes that were bold and warm as if radiating some heat through the paper. In the photo he was smiling as if Casper had just told an embarrassing joke in the typical Dad style. The website seemed to have decided that Daniel would develop a small freckle below his right eye. Casper printed off the final image, turned it over and wrote a final message.

3

Perhaps this is the man you are today. I
made this because I wanted to know what I
was missing. Aren't you handsome? I wish I
could've been around to watch you become
this man. I promise to enjoy my time with
you as a baby as much as possible. I hope
you smile like you do here when you find
this. I just wanted to leave something behind
so that you would know how much I was
thinking of you and your future in this
moment.

He sealed the photo and letter in a large envelope, and
then put it on top of the last will and testament papers
he had been mulling over. When you're aware of your
impending death there always seems to be a lot of paper-
work involved. The messy, sudden deaths always seem
a lot easier on the person who died. Casper, however,
seemed to be more focused on planning the intricacies of
his own funeral and dividing his assets than living those
remaining days without hassle. The letter, now sealed,
was placed on the side of his desk and very swiftly for-
gotten about.

*

Twenty years later Danielle found the letter amongst a
box of her mother's possessions. Inside was a photo of
the man she should, no, would have been. Printed before
her was the cruel reminder of the body she had been
born into. She looked down at the face, so familiar but
so distant, and fell silent. This was a different person to
the artificially purple-haired woman with razor sharp

cheekbones and lusciously plump lips holding the photo. Having only returned to the home of her late mother to handle her affairs, she had never expected this. Danielle tugged at her dress awkwardly and impulsively as if to cover up the flesh to hide her past self. How was her father to have known that Danielle grew up indulging in tea parties, fancy dress and experimentation with eye-liner long before her long transition into womanhood? Picking up a nearby red pen with her chest heaving and her eyes welling up with unruly tears, Danielle scrawled a note beneath the message her father left, a small smile escaping her lips as she did.

> Dear Dad,
> I know you meant well by your letter, but
> I feel we have much to catch up on. I miss
> you. I have always missed you and lamented
> this Dad shaped void within my life but it
> has been a good life. I'm hoping I still man-
> aged to make you proud. I wish you could
> have been around too but my milestones
> have been somewhat different than what
> you probably expected. I really hope we will
> get to sit down and discuss it one day.

A Call In
The Night

AFTER A THIRD sleepless night Lydia decided that it was time to put her demons to rest. As the digital clock on the table hit '2:00' Lydia pressed the receiver against her pale lips. Holding the telephone between her face and her shoulder, she fumbled her hand about the inside of her bag. Lydia pulled out the crumpled piece of paper, located at the bottom of the bag amongst lip gloss smears and discarded pennies, and smoothed it out. She found the flyer, printed in purple lettering. The small, creased piece of paper offered a potentially exciting new experience.

Dream Circuit: A Radio show like no other!

Every Sunday at 2am if you call up we'll connect you with a stranger to discuss your dreams. You remain completely anonymous.

The idea is to openly discuss dreams and nightmares with the stranger in the hopes that it will be an almost therapeutic experience. When you're done simply hang up the phone and no one ever need know you spoke at all. We do not take or distribute any personal information. This service is entirely free.

Call up.

Sweet Dreams

Below this was a phone number. Lydia dialled in the number and heard the cold ring-out tone, like the cold purr of a cat. Eventually an operator picked up.

'Hello,' the voice said, 'Just hold for a moment please. We'll connect you with a stranger any moment now.'

The predictable 'on hold' music began. The sound of a slightly out of tune piano poured through the tinny sound quality of the phone and Lydia took this moment to finish making her mug of tea. Pouring water from the kettle into the mug, she heard a voice, low and dull. She jumped at the sound, splashing boiling water over the avocado laminate counter-tops.

'Hello?'

'Yes, hello?'

Something churned in her stomach. Perhaps it was a response to the strangeness of the situation. Here she was on the phone with an absolute stranger in the hopes of discussing something so intimate that only she had experienced it. There was a moment when the two of them, strangers in the night, said nothing. Lydia forced herself to find courage and spoke.

'So,' Lydia murmured, 'Who goes first?'

'Well,' the voice said, 'You sound like a lady so why not go with the old 'ladies first' rule?'

Lydia was more than happy to do so.

'Ok,' she said as she carried her mug over to the sofa and pulled a blanket over herself. She wore only a white night dress, having been unable to sleep, and kept one hand pressed down on the mug in an attempt to absorb some warmth.

'I'm calling because I keep having the same dream,' she explained. She was speaking to a faceless person in some tenuous third space between the realms of 'here' and 'there' and it all felt a little absurd. She was allowing a stranger full access to the images only she had seen, the cave paintings on the inside of her cavernous skull, and letting him wander with her through the imagery.

'Three nights in a row now I've had this dream. The first part of the dream I'm climbing. I find myself climbing concrete stairs, cold on my bare feet, and light is pouring through the windows which I never stop to look out of. My ascension is slow and seemingly tiring. I notice my arms are covered in writing like the pages of a book. For some reason I cannot read the letters...'

Lydia trailed off as she traced her fingers around the edge of the mug, her fingers dancing around the traces of steam.

'Then I come to a grey door ahead of me. Pushing it open, I realise I'm on the roof of a building I've never been to. I walk out onto the roof and the floor is flooded, water everywhere. Everything seems almost completely silent apart from the occasional bird call from out in the distance. Then, ahead of me, I notice several people all hunched around a table. The table is littered with smashed, foodless plates. They're playing some sort of card game but all their cards are blank. It is at this moment I realise their faces are blank too. Their eyes are carved out holes, their mouths mere slits, and yet I sense that they are looking at me.'

Lydia shuddered as she remembered those hollow faces.

'One offers me an outstretched hand. At first I'm cautious. Then the rest of the faceless people stand and begin to scuttle hither and thither as if to block the path I had entered from. The faceless being leads me to the edge and wordlessly points me to the horizon. I follow; my trust is absolute in that moment. There I see the sun, but it's not a sun, it's more like a large egg cracked and frying upon the acid green and magenta infused horizon. In the sky around me fish swim as if the air itself was made of water. I realise, at this point, that I'm not breathing. I haven't been the whole dream.'

Lydia paused for a moment, taking a sip of tea and drinking the roses back into her pale cheeks. There was a long pause, not exactly a silence since the static crackle of the phone line remained, but Lydia wondered if the stranger had gone or hung up.

The voice on the line asked, 'What next?'

'Then, around the town, bells start to chime. One at first, then two and then the ringing is all I can hear.'

Lydia paused. Everything she was saying sounded absurd and she knew it. She felt her thumb twitch as if begging to hang up, saving herself from this embarrassment. She then decided that she'd already confessed enough. She may as well follow through with her confession. If she could just get this off her chest perhaps she'd sleep soundly as a result. After a deep breath she continues her tale.

'Deafening, maddening chimes and rain begins to fall... or rise. That's when it begins to rain upwards.'

10

Lydia expected some interest from the person on the other end of the line, a follow up question perhaps to indicate some level of interest, but heard only the soft murmur of breathing like the wings of a butterfly. She found it almost offensive that the stranger didn't seem interested. She had certainly thought it interesting enough. Lydia decided to continue to talk. Perhaps if she discussed this dream fully it would stop altogether.

'And then something happens... at that point I topple forward and I'm falling down the side of the building towards the pavement below. I fall with grace for a moment, casting myself into pirouettes and a delicate demi-plié, en pointe but with no floor to balance upon. I hear the chiming of clocks that become louder the closer I get to the floor. Beneath I notice a congregation of wolves, dressed in suits and mouths stained crimson, and know they are waiting for me. I hear them howl and growl. Their eyes, ravenous and sharp, gaze through me expectantly.'

No response came. Perhaps the person on the other end of the tenuous link that a telephone call provided had lost interest. Her confession was nearly over. She had almost relieved herself entirely.

'The fall lasts some time and all I can hear is the ringing, the call of birds and the laughter from those above. I hit the pavement and feel blood pooling around my eyes, in my ears, from my nose. I can even taste it on my tongue. Everything around me begins to dissolve and disintegrate but I, unable to move, can only watch the world around me vanish. The fish swirl upwards with the rain and the buildings turn to ash and rise like flames. Something, perhaps the air, tears the wolves apart. First they are torn from their clothing. Then they are ripped limb from limb as they ascend upwards. I remain. Then,

11

when all is gone, all that is left is my bloody and mangled body left entirely alone. I wake up and I can feel pain where, in the dream, I hit the ground.'

A breeze outside whistled past as if to serve as a reminder that the world outside was fine. Lydia broke from her train of thought.

'I'm sorry,' Lydia said, 'I've dominated the conversation. Tell me about your dreams. You must be tired of hearing mine.'

She felt foolish for opening up so much. Surely most people have such dreams and hers probably made her sound crazy. She ran her slender fingers carelessly through her hair.

'Not at all,' the voice said, 'Though it *is* funny...'
'What is?'

'Because, Lydia, I dream of pushing you.'

Creep

Y OU'D PROBABLY THINK I was a creep or something. I'm not, I'm not, I'm really not! I just love her, that's all. In fact there's nothing wrong with loving someone – especially someone who means so much to you, someone who *saved you* in a way. *Sarah.* That's her name and I love her more than anything. I suppose the only real problem is that someone got there before I did. *John.* John is her husband and I often overhear (I'm not eavesdropping – I'm not!) them talk by the car as they both prepare to depart for work, reminding each other of how much they love the other. It's heartbreaking. I feel deeply that I should be the only object of her affection. I'm old now, very old... My joints are weak and my hips aren't what they used to be anymore so is it any wonder that I long for some sort of affection in my golden days? Is it sad that whenever she goes away to work or to the shops or to visit someone I genuinely sit by the window and I pine the day away until she comes back? Yeah, that's probably a bit sad. When she is away at work I sneak into her room. There's something comforting about being surrounded by her scent. I notice a pair of her pants on the floor and within seconds, without thinking, they're in my mouth clasped between my teeth. I hold them there for a moment before plunging myself onto her bed. Rolling around in the sheets I drown myself in the scent of *her*. It clings to me for the rest of the day and leaves me feeling content. One day I snuck into her room and rubbed myself all over her sheets mingling my scent with hers upon the fabric, wishing I could sleep here at her side. It was at that moment that I leapt up, hearing the door behind me scrape open, and I realised.

I'd been caught.

I expected the worst as I looked at John but was relieved when he merely smiled and said 'Oh Dylan, what are you doing here? Is this because I haven't taken you on your walkies today? Come on then, you silly dog...'

One

There is one love that is stronger than all others. No, it is not that between two lovers nor that felt between a child and a parent. It's the love between siblings. I don't quite know what it is. You start in the same place, you share a womb, you come from the same fleshy beginning and thus you are bonded. My dear brother and I, however, were more bonded than most. When cut from our failing mother's body the doctor practically dropped us back in. He'd never seen anything like it. Twins – but joined down the side. So close to being 'perfectly' formed, but a section of our flesh made us conjoined. Where my right arm, and his left of course, should have been there was no arm, just the seam that ran down our sides joining our two middle-legs, not sure where one truly ended and the other began.

'Well,' father said, attempting to utilise humour to break the silence, 'They'll beat all the other boys in the three-legged race.'

It was the last joke father ever made. There's not much for a man to laugh about once his wife dies of shame thinking she'd birthed a monster. Before our forced removal from her pitiful womb had we not been the perfect sons? Two for the price of one, squished down into one body, travel size I suppose you could call us. Two, yet One. I am the twin on the left, or the right if you're looking at me, the left head, or right if you're looking; not that you'd be looking. Everyone always looks away. I couldn't bear the loneliness that other humans must experience. My brother and I are so often seen as freaks, but I believe we are superior. We hold a kind of kinship that other humans could not. We were better by far.

My brother held such contempt for all those who saw us as anything different. I can assure you that I did not see it in the same way. I had one arm and one leg to myself, my other leg was shared. Had anyone ever opened us up to examine our organs I dread to think what they would have found. I grew up praying to have my own organs. Some twins or siblings fight over toys, don't they? My brother and I fought over organs. Though I love him, I have spent so much of life being tired of his views. At times my mind would show me my biggest dream: a large razor that swooped down, slicing us right down the middle, the shameful freak no more, my own man. Of course people would stare at an amputee, I was so used to having my own one arm that I'd adjust rather quickly, but amputees are more acceptable. Years of dreaming and I finally started to think: what if? What if the separation could be done? Though waking each morning I felt a twinge of fear, never quite knowing if my brother could see the same dreams as me, never quite sure how exactly 'to myself' I ever was.

I'm sure you're wondering, dear reader, how our life was. How did we manage? As toddlers we fed ourselves, and each other, wondering which stomach it would go into. Did we have one stomach? Two? Oh, the fascination of it all. We were a perpetual mystery, not only to those around us, but also to ourselves and that made each day fascinating. We were homeschooled; father demanded it. His shame had made it mandatory. I suppose we were the funniest little thing, a gaggle of heads and limbs, a writhing mess of our entwined insides, it's all rather poetic. There's nothing better than the feeling that you'll never spend a day alone.

Betrayal is the last thing that I expected, dear brother. It is something for which I shall never forgive you. In taking yourself, you took me. Every part of what is you was part of what is me. There can be no greater theft.

I never had any time alone. Growing up and dating was out of the question. My brother would have been a third wheel, and I to him, so as teens we never had a girlfriend; only each other. Some days I didn't mind, and other times I longed for companionship. It was disturbing though; we came to the point when the body has urges that long to be explored in ways that one is to do alone. I was never alone. My brother would often sit each night, awake and creating pleasure, and I'd feel a strange feeling of horror as I could feel the full tremor of each motion too. It was as if I was sharing in his personal pleasure and it sickened me. There are things brothers are not meant to share. It felt like I lived ten years or so of unwilling incest, but I'd have to remind myself that it wasn't incest if you shared the same skin.

Sometimes when one brain rests, the other is wide awake. Often as my brother slept, I would sit awake all night. One evening, as my brother slept at my side, I read a newspaper that father had left on the dining room table. Trying to find solace in the blotches of words, I noticed a rather relevant article about a radical doctor in the next city along who had separated twins joined at the head. Both of them had survived. Not for too long, but I suppose when you're joined at the head there is more at risk. A strange pang of excitement rose in our stomach. I made a phone call, fingers trembling as each cold ring of the phone echoed for what felt like an age until the woman at the other end, her voice cold and clinical, responded. I booked us in for the next morning. As the waxy half moon faded, the sky gave birth to a crimson dawn and the sun rose over the arching line of the horizon, I proposed that my brother and I take the bus over to the city to see the sights. He agreed. With a body like ours it is hard not to. If one goes, the other follows. The bus ride over there was so uncomfortable, but I considered that it would hopefully be the final awkward encounter I'd ever have to endure. Arriving in the city, I spotted the hospital and dragged my brother there. Thankfully, I'm

the stronger boy. The doctor's office, cold and stinking of chemicals that burned my nostril hair, felt like a wondrous place. My brother kept kicking, but I held still, controlling our middle-leg. I needed all my strength.

My all-too-sweet brother dragged us into the office, the doctor sat before us, staring at our strained frame. His hands were clasped, his speech full of 'Mmmm' and 'Ahhh' as if he were feigning some level of understanding. I'd rather take a cold, hard enema than listen to people pretend to understand. They talked. I sat in disbelief as my brother spoke of a promise made whilst I'd been sleeping. He had promised the doctor half of any money he made through his entire life if he were to split us regardless of my consent. Greed welled up in the doctor's eyes, the dollar signs practically rising in his pupils. He quickly ordered a nurse in who came over to us, the silver point of the needle in the syringe pointed at me. A jab! My surroundings faded into nothingness.

I was alone, tingles jabbing at what had been our middle, but now was my side. By the time I woke up my brother was gone. According to the nurse that came to aid me, my brother had the raw end of the deal. When they separated our 'middle-leg' into the two legs they were 'meant to be' my leg had full function, my brother had suffered some nerve damage and his newly 'free' leg couldn't be moved and he was whizzing around the hospital in a wheelchair.

My brother left me in that damned hospital, and ran away for five years. He claimed it was 'soul searching' or some bollocks like that. He'd send postcards. Not the 'Wish you were here' kind, but ones with bleak landscapes from bland towns no one truly cares for. How much soul searching can you do in the middle of nowhere? He was showing off. I know it. All I came to learn is that he found someone and settled down; an ex-soldier, an amputee as a result of a bomb blast whilst out on active duty. I got the strange feeling that my brother had not told her about me. There was no suggestion of me or father visiting, no warm wishes. He probably told her he lost his limbs in some sort of traffic accident and spared her the truth, the spineless cunt.

My waking body felt sore but a lot lighter than ever before. I sat up slowly with more ease than ever: I didn't have to negotiate with my brother's body. He lay beside me in a separate bed. The space between us felt like oceans, continents. Like freedom.

Whirling around the hospital the nurses had to tell me to slow down, worried that I'd exhaust myself. I told them that I was the happiest I'd ever been, begging to leave the hospital before my poor brother woke up. I was sure he'd be unhappy. With the way we had been raised, coming to a junction in our lives like this and facing the decision to be separated, I suppose only one of us could be happy. I was sure my brother would adjust to it all. Hell – I figured that soon he would be as cheerful as I was about the whole ordeal. I was looking forward to a life of bathing alone. Lord, I'd be able to fit into a bathtub, I thought. I could date a woman without my brother as a third wheel – I could have sex. Bloody hell – I could have as much sex as I wanted as soon as I learned how to.

Eventually my brother sent mail informing us of where he lived, inviting us to some sort of Christmas dinner. I had not heard from my father for some time. Not because I had not seen him, we still lived in the same house, we just co-existed in a manner where he didn't have to be reminded of my existence. Why shouldn't he love me now? I was as dull and lonely as him. My scars were simply external. I was the only one to reply to the card. I took him up on the offer immediately.

The night before Christmas I came to the house of my brother and his woman. Their home seemed like the typical portrait of domestic bliss, everything in the house having come in pieces from IKEA, lacking in any sort of originality. We ate, we drank, I spent most of my time looking at the Nativity Scene set up in the corner, everyone bowing to the little Christ, a dull, China figurine painted in beige and white, dull as fuck. My mind flashed straight to his end, the crucifixion. That bit I liked. I imagined the wise men around the manger driving nails through the baby's hands and feet, the bones snapping like twigs and poking out of the tattered ruins at the ends of his arms. Then I thought of the needle. I still have nightmares about needles, the spear in Christ's side.

They provided me with a wheelchair and crutches so I could leave as soon as possible. Did I feel wrong about leaving my brother behind? Of course I did. But did I want to face him in his waking fury? Certainly not! To flee was my only option, at least until my brother calmed down and learned to forgive me. I felt that leaving him to his own meditation was the best thing to do at this stage. I didn't expect to be gone as long as I was.

The sex was awkward by normal standards I suppose, but it was the first I'd ever known and so I had no reason to not enjoy it. We'd lumber our broken bodies together, dragging our limbs into place and pushing our bodies into position. She would run her fingers down my seam, the scar that ran from shoulder to ankle. It was as if we had been made broken, but able to fit so perfectly with each other. My useless leg could sit where her amputated leg ended – at least we had a pair of working legs between us. Pushing my working leg against the base of the bed I would begin to rise and thrust slowly as they did in the movies but with one arm propping me up like an awkward set of push-ups ending in a shuddering crescendo. This woman, now my wife, understood me. She looked at me with no disgust, simply love and sympathy. We shared wounds and hurts that the other could understand and we could provide what the other physically lacked. A pair of interlocking, broken dolls.

Father had warned me that my dear brother had never quite recovered from the fulcrum of our lives, the great separation that had freed us as men. Hardly seeing it as freedom, he saw it as betrayal and had become bitter, internalising every ache and pain as something that I had caused. My invitation for a Christmas meal was my way of apologising. I could not bring myself to regret my decision, but I'd always hold his hatred for the backhanded deal that brought that fate upon us.

27

For years I'd dreamed of needles. The cold needle that jabbed me asleep, ending my superhuman existence played on my mind, and now needles were all I thought of. They are jabbing, prying, cold things. The lonely seam down my side tingled for so long after it felt like needles and I a mere puppet that had been opened up, pushed full of stuffing, and sewn together once more. I was a puppet. A fucking puppet. Do you know that people who have two hands have more than the average number of hands? Because, you know, if you take into consideration that some people out there have one hand, or no hands, Hell – maybe three hands, that alters the data somewhat. Amputees, when added to the mixture, make two handed people above average. Now who's to say you can't be even better than that? Three legs! Two heads! I wanted the rest of my fucking body back. I kept having the same nightmare over and over, bits of my body getting up, walking away and leaving me. My hands would hop off, waltzing off as if the fat little fingers were legs, the nails tap-tap-tapping on the floor like some fancy stilettos. Then my lips would hop off and slither away, kissing the ground as they went. Bit by bit my body parts would go until there was nothing left of me but memories. Then there he was, dear brother of mine, standing in the doorway of my dreams as my body parts made their little pilgrimage towards his new form, leaving me for him.

The little woman, my brother's pet, was in the kitchen cleaning the dishes. She tipped the carcass of the turkey, stripped bare to the bone, into the trashcan, discarding all the smaller bones that had been torn and divided onto everyone's plate. 'Are you a breast man or a leg man?' she asked me, chuckling as her plump cheeks became rosy. She and my brother carved the turkey together, each offering their only arm to do the task together, his seam-side pressed against her. We talked some, then made our excuses to all head to bed, my brother staying downstairs. He was sitting in an armchair, crutches propped up beside it, 'Oh Holy Night' came the voices of carollers floating in from the nearby village churchyard, 'It is the night of our dear Saviour's birth.'

I find the best way to silence someone is to hit them with a heavy object.

Several times.

'Brother,' I said, having looked up after hearing soft footsteps behind me, 'Can you not sleep? Won't you say something? I... what are you doing? Put down the lamp or...'

Quite some time later I recall my eyes fluttering open. I was home, but down in the basement sprawled on my workbench. I could tell this initially by the chill, then the bright and unyielding light swinging a little above my head. My head was pounding, dizzy, as if I'd been sedated, but certainly not properly. I could smell blood and knew it was my own. I heard the sound of metal on metal, clanking and scratching. Unsettled, I tried to call out but couldn't quite seem to move my tongue.

Putting needle and thread to flesh in an attempt to right wrongs and rejoin, I felt it sting as I first pushed the needle through the skin, starting at the bottom, working upwards.

My brother tried to moan and cry out. Afraid that someone would hear, I gave him another good whack to the head. Ah, silence. I had to pick up speed so I worked the needle in faster and faster making messy work but progress nonetheless. I began to pant, my breathing quickening as my heartbeat started to race beneath our chest, continuing the sacred work. It wasn't the join we were born into but for now this would have to do. Once I got to our shoulders I couldn't quite turn my head to see, working blindly, stabbing wherever I felt the need to. The sweet sting of unity cried out with our blood, the stigmatic little marks like crimson vows of old promises renewed. Making quick work of tying off the thread, I tossed the needle aside without care of where it landed. I threw my head back, closing my eyes and letting the back of my head hit the table. This was as close to perfect as we could be for now, unified once more, closer than close and thicker than family, we were One once more.

I rolled my head onto the space beneath us, not quite neck and not quite shoulder but us, and there I rested for a moment, breathing it in. My brother had a new smell to him, perhaps some French cologne from the wife that I didn't quite like as it didn't suit our body. It reeked of a pretentiousness I didn't care for. That would have to go now.

'I know you want me to be sorry,' I told him, 'But I'm not. Neither were you at the separation, remember? So for that I make no apologies. This is our birth right, brother. You wanted the experience of what? Loneliness?

Is that what you sought? Well you've had your fun, and everything can return to normal now, can't it?'

My words came roughly as I was panting after having made rather quick work of it all. I found myself waiting for his response and expecting his typical whiney drone.

'Brother?'

I could just about move my head. Then I felt a sudden warmth at my side and heard that all too familiar voice.

'Back to how it's meant to be,' and I felt my brother squirming at my side, trying to become level with me, matching our seams together. Dear God...

'Brother? Say something, you old bastard.'

Turning my head, I looked at him. His face was paler now. I cast my gaze downwards. The little dots that tracked up our joint had spewed forth reddish drops that were now drying, turning a murky brown. His had darkened some time ago and stopped bleeding. I shook us, his head lolling about like a doll. His hair fell back and I saw the marks on his head, purple and blotchy like paint stains, spotted and smeared with the brownish stains of dried blood, flecks of crimson within it too as if the blood willed itself to remain fresh. Perhaps I'd hit him a bit too hard. I started to wonder if it mattered whether or not his lungs filled with air or his eyes opened. Mine were working enough for the rest of our body. I was the core now, our support system and I would live enough for the both of us, I was sure of it. As long as we were One I didn't quite care about anything else. So we lay there, unified, One as the snowflakes fell outside, unique as we.